KATIE

THE REVOLTING WEDDING

Katie

THE REVOLTING WEDDING

MARY HOOPER

ILLUSTRATIONS BY

FREDERIQUE VAYSSIERE

BLOOMSBURY

Published in Great Britain in 2007 by Bloomsbury Publishing Plc
36 Soho Square, London, W1D 3QY

First published in the UK by Blackie and Son Ltd, 1992

A CIP catalogue record of this book is available from the
British Library

ISBN 978 0 7475 8612 8

Printed in Great Britain by Clays Ltd, St Ives Plc

1 3 5 7 9 10 8 6 4 2

All papers used by Bloomsbury Publishing are natural, recyclable products made
from wood grown in well-managed forests. The manufacturing processes conform to
the environmental regulations of the country of origin.

Typeset by Dorchester Typesetting Group Ltd

www.maryhooper.co.uk
www.bloomsbury.com/childrens

chapter one

'When do we have to put them on?' Flicka asked, jabbing a finger towards the whisper blue bridesmaids' dresses hanging on my wardrobe door. She poked at a bit of exquisite beading. 'Have you ever *seen* anything so revolting?'

I shook my head. 'Never.'

'I mean, she couldn't have found anything more gross if she'd tried.'

I shot a look at the dresses, hanging there in all their frilliness and soppiness. 'I expect she *did* try. She probably went to the Brides' Boutique place and said that none of the dresses were *quite* revolting enough so . . .'

'. . . could they kindly do her something that was *considerably* more awful,' Flicka finished in Mrs Bayleaf's voice.

I grinned. Mrs Bayleaf's real name was Mrs Bailey and she was Flicka's aunt. She was also the mother of a man called Christopher, and my sister Helen was marrying this Christopher at three o'clock – in spite of all my efforts to get her to change her mind.

As we stood glowering at the dresses there was a ring at the doorbell. 'That's Mum back from the hairdressers, I expect,' I said. 'Coming down?'

She nodded and we raced and scrambled to get out of the bedroom door first. I generously let her win, not just because Mum had told me to be nice to her, but because she – Flicka – was much better than I'd thought she was going to be. Well, Mrs

Bayleaf had described her as a delightful blond-haired little angel, so I was expecting someone foul, but now that I'd met her it was all right.

I slid down the bannisters and Flicka went down head first, slithering and sliding like an eel. We arrived at the bottom at the same time and I forward-rolled on to the *Welcome* mat and flung the door open.

It wasn't Mum, though. It was Mrs Bayleaf in her wedding outfit: a barrel of pink chiffon under a coat of pink chiffon topped by a hat of pink chiffon. It looked as if she'd got caught in one of those

candy-floss-making machines at the fair and it had spun out of control.

I gawped at all her pinkness. Flicka got up quickly and we both stood to attention.

'Katie . . . Felicity . . .' Mrs Bayleaf said as we tried to brush bits of carpet off us. 'Not dressed yet?'

'We . . . er . . .' I began.

'They're such beautiful dresses that we can't bear to put them on in case we crease them,' Flicka said earnestly.

'So we were just sitting quietly on the end of the bed admiring them!' I finished.

'Quite so,' Mrs Bayleaf said, pleased. 'Is your mother in, dear?'

I shook my head. 'She's at the hairdressers.'

She looked at my hair hopefully. 'And you'll be going to the hairdressers too, will you?'

'I've been banned,' I said. 'I went with Mum once and mixed up the perm solution with the bleach solution and . . .'

'Never mind, dear.' She turned her attention to Flicka. 'But whatever's happened to your lovely curls?' She frowned deeply, looked Flicka up and down – her tracksuit was almost as awful as mine. 'You look quite . . . quite different.'

'Oh, the curls will come back,' Flicka said, waggling the elastic band her hair was scraped into.

'One sincerely hopes so, dear.' Mrs Bayleaf suddenly delved into the Bliss Department Store carrier bag she was holding. 'But I mustn't stop – I just came to bring you both a surprise!'

I nudged Flicka, she nudged me back. We both knew that a Mrs Bayleaf surprise wasn't going to be a decent one.

'Ta-ra!' she trumpeted, and she brought out two revolting little draw-string bag things and dangled them from her fingers. They were a bit like loo roll covers and a bit like small lampshades – and with a shudder I noticed that they were whisper blue, with exquisite beading . . .

'Dorothy bags to match your bridesmaids' dresses!' she trilled. 'For you to carry your little essentials to church.'

'How awfu—' I began.

'Awfully lovely!' Flicka interrupted quickly.

'Aren't they!' she beamed. 'And they're both the same, so no arguments.'

Grudgingly, reluctantly, we took them.

'You're allowed to keep them after the wedding,' she said. 'Just think how handy they'll be for taking things to school!'

Flicka and I were speechless – she must have thought we were speechless with delight because she added, 'I knew you'd love them! I said to my Cedric that I'd keep them until this morning – just one more little treat for you!'

'They're amazing,' I said truthfully.

'Incredible,' Flicka agreed.

A simpering look crossed over Mrs Bayleaf's over-powdered face. 'And how is the blushing bride?' she asked coyly.

'Oh . . . er . . . much the same,' I said. I hadn't seen much of Helen, actually – she'd been shut in her room, giggling with two friends half the morning.

Mr Bayleaf, still in the car, beeped his horn. 'Well, mustn't stop, dears,' Mrs Bayleaf said. 'A thousand things to do!' She beamed one last smile and retreated down the path in a pink cloud.

I slammed the door and Flicka and I rolled our eyes at each other.

'Overkill on the pink, I think.'

'*Dorothy* bags!'

'Grrr-*oss* or what!'

Whirling them round our heads, we went into the kitchen.

'All this food!' Flicka said, eyes goggling as she looked at the turkey and the whale-sized salmon and the millions of pastry thingies.

'And none of it to eat!' I said.

'What's it for, then?'

'Well, it's not to eat *now*, I mean. You know

we're going to the hotel for the wedding breakfast bit?'

She nodded.

'Well, that's just for forty people – close friends and relatives. Tonight, when Helen and Christopher have gone off on their honeymoon, loads of people are coming back here for a party.'

Flicka rubbed her tummy. 'Couldn't we just have a little pastry whatsit?'

'Oh, I should think so,' I said airily. 'No one's going to notice.' I took four big square things, gave her two. 'Do you want to come and see the cake?' I asked. 'I think it's in the dining room – unless Dad's already taken it along to the hotel.'

We went into the dining room, swinging our Dorothy bags. The cake was still there, a towering monstrosity of shiny white icing with a simpering bride and groom stuck on top. 'Those blue bits around the top are bluebirds of happiness,' I explained. 'Blue and white – Mrs Bayleaf says that's our wedding's *theme* colour.'

'Oh yes?' Flicka said, unimpressed.

I showed her the small hole where I'd eaten a lump of icing. 'I had to, I was starving to death,'

I said. 'We haven't had a proper meal in this house for *months*; everyone's been too busy doing things for the wedding.'

Flicka was on one side of the table, I was on the other. We started throwing the Dorothy bags backwards and forwards over the top of the cake.

'I was practically reduced to hunting in the dustbins!' I went on, the bags whizzing about quicker and quicker. 'Even the cat's left home.'

Flicka grinned. She had both the bags and flung them to me one after the other. I caught one, lunged for the next one – and then it happened:

the Great Disaster. Somehow my foot went sideways and I fell forward – *right on to the wedding cake*. The little bride and groom tumbled off the top and the three tiers collapsed on to each other. The small top cake landed upside down on the table and the middle one broke completely in half, showering the whole room with currants, bits of white icing, little silver horseshoes and bluebirds of happiness.

I screamed. Flicka screamed – and then the doorbell rang.

It was Mum back from the hairdressers.

chapter two

I nearly burst out crying but I was too scared to. I'd been frozen to bits with fright.

'Whatever are you going to *do*?' Flicka asked in a quavery voice.

'I'm going to get *killed*, that's what,' I quavered back.

We stared at the disaster area in front of us. Bits of icing lay like snow over half the dining room, the little bride and groom had nosedived on to the carpet and the columns that had supported the top two tiers had rolled under the table.

The front door bell went again but I could only flap my hands and make squeaky panic noises.

'What shall we *do*?' Flicka asked urgently. 'Try to pick it up and stick it together?'

'Don't . . . don't know . . .' I stammered.

From upstairs came a yell from Helen, demanding that I go and answer the door.

'Look,' I said to Flicka desperately. 'We'll let my mum in and then we'll try to keep her out of here while I think of what to do. Right?'

'Right,' Flicka said. 'But unless you can somehow bake and ice another cake in ten minutes I reckon you might as well start packing your suitcase.'

We let Mum in – Mum with a hugely big and bouncy hairdo.

I stared at her. 'Your hair looks funny,' I said.

'Thank you, Katie,' she said. 'I can always rely on you to make me feel good.' She inspected me closely. 'You look quite pale. I expect it's all the excitement.'

'I expect so,' I said. 'Mum . . . this is Felicity. She likes to be called Flicka.'

'Hello, Flicka,' Mum said. She looked a bit taken aback. 'You're not at all how I thought you'd be – we were expecting a little golden-haired angel, weren't we, Katie?'

'Yes. Isn't it good?' I said. 'Mum, Flicka . . . er . . . wants to show you something upstairs. *Don't* you?' I said pointedly to Flicka.

'All in good time,' Mum said, trying to get past

me into the dining room. 'I've got to get the cake parcelled up for Dad to take to the hotel and then there's a million and one things to be done before three o'clock.'

I stayed glued across the dining-room door so she couldn't get by. 'But Flicka desperately wants to show you . . . to show you . . .' I cast around for a reason, '. . . wants to show you her amazing song and dance routines!' I finished.

'Do you, Flicka?' asked Mum.

'Do I?' Flicka said in amazement.

'Yes!' I said. 'She wants to do a song and dance act at the reception. To entertain everyone.'

'Oh, yes, so I do,' Flicka said faintly. 'I'd almost forgotten.'

'Well, she can sing and dance later in the kitchen and show me there,' Mum said.

'No! It's got to be done upstairs! She's got to do it upstairs for you properly where . . . where there's more space,' I said desperately.

'I really haven't got . . .' Mum began.

I pulled Mum to one side. 'You'll have to,' I whispered. 'She's very temperamental . . . *very*. She had hysterics when I said I didn't want to see it.

You'll *have* to go and watch her or she'll start screaming and crying and carrying on.'

Mum, startled, took a step backwards. 'All right,' she said soothingly to Flicka. 'We'll go upstairs now and you can show me your *lovely* song and dance act. All right?'

'Yes, thank you, Mrs Wilkins,' Flicka said, rolling her eyes at me.

Once they'd gone up I dashed into the dining room. If anything, the Great Cake Disaster looked even worse . . . even more disastrous. Maybe, I thought, if I could just get all the bits back into the boxes so it could be taken to the hotel, then I'd have a chance of getting away with it. If the cake was discovered all broken to bits *once it was there*, well, *that* could have happened on the journey.

Quickly, carefully, I picked up everything – all the decent-sized bits, anyway – and put them into the three big white boxes that the cake had come in from the shop. Most of the icing had fallen off the top tier and the middle one had broken completely in half, but the bottom tier looked pretty

reasonable – that is, reasonable if you were pre-pared to overlook the big cracks all down the sides, the oozing-out marzipan and the bluebirds of happiness with no heads.

I finished packing the boxes, folded down the lids, carefully swept the floor and hid all the bits in newspaper in the dustbin, and then went upstairs where I could hear Flicka singing 'God Save the Queen' rather desperately.

I had my hand on my bedroom door when I suddenly looked down at myself and almost had a heart attack: I was covered in wedding cake! The bobbles on my tracksuit had somehow picked up bits of icing, there was a yellow sticky bit of marzipan stuck on my knee and currants decorat-ed my sleeves.

I didn't know what to do; all my other clothes were in my bedroom. If I went in as I was, though, it would be a dead give-away . . .

Thirty seconds later I pushed open the door. Flicka, on the first line of 'Happy Birthday to You', looked surprised but relieved to see me. Mum shook her head and gave a loud tut.

'Whatever are you *doing*, Katie?' she said. 'Why

are you walking around the house just wearing your underwear?'

I pretended to fan myself. 'It's so hot in here!' I said. 'I felt quite faint. I just had to get my track-suit off or I'd have died of heat poisoning.'

'Don't be ridiculous!' Mum said, sighing. 'Honestly, sometimes I wonder if you're quite all right.' She moved towards the door. 'Well, those were lovely songs, Felicity, but I'm really not sure that 'You're a Pink Toothbrush' and 'The Billy Goat Gruff Song' will go down all that well at the wedding reception.'

'Oh, all right then, if you're sure,' Flicka said.

Mum went out, looking rather dazed, then reappeared a few seconds later. 'You two needn't put your bridesmaids' dresses on until the last moment,' she said, 'just in case anything happens to them.'

'OK!' we said happily.

'And Katie – you will behave yourself today, won't you?'

'Of course I will,' I said indignantly.

'I've got terrible misgivings,' she said, shaking her head, 'and I'm not at all sure that bribes work, but just to show willing: you know that trampoline you've always wanted?'

'The garden-sized one?' I asked.

'Yes,' she said. 'Well, if you're wonderfully, perfectly good all day, then we're going to buy it for you.'

'Fantastic!' I said, for a moment forgetting the Great Cake Disaster.

Mum waggled her finger at me. 'But I do mean wonderfully, perfectly good every single minute of the day. And you can start by putting some clothes on.'

She went out and I flopped on to the bed and sighed. 'I've *always* wanted a trampoline,' I said mournfully, 'but I haven't got a hope of getting it.'

Flicka moved to the window. 'Just as long as I haven't got to distract a hotelful of wedding guests by singing to them when the cake appears . . .' She pointed outside. 'There's a man getting out of a car with a crate of bottles. Is it your dad?'

I jumped up and looked out: it was.

'Right!' I said, searching for my number two tracksuit in the fluff under the bed. 'Let's go!'

'Where?'

'To the hotel with dad to deliver the cake,' I said. 'And on the way there we've got to try to push the cake boxes on to the floor!'

Flicka looked at me nervously. 'There's no chance of me staying here quietly on my own, I suppose?'

'Of course not!' I said. 'We're in this together.'

She sighed. 'I thought you might say that.'

chapter three

I put on my tracksuit and then Flicka and I leapt downstairs to make sure Dad didn't try to look in the cake boxes. We'd got halfway down when Helen, with what looked like pink mud on her face, put her head out of her bedroom and said I was to ask Mum to come up straight away as she'd had a disaster.

'What sort of a disaster?' I asked, interested.

'Never you mind,' she said.

It was the way she said it; for a moment I felt quite hopeful. 'Have you gone off him?' I asked. 'If so, it's not too late to change your mind. I can help Dad take the cake back and –'

'Don't be so ridiculous,' she snapped. 'Just tell Mum that I've broken my fingernail, will you?'

I made a 'pshaw' sort of noise. 'Call that a disaster?' I said. 'A disaster is when something *disastrous* happens like someone falls on a wedd—'

Flicka dug me in the back. 'Come on!' she interrupted. 'I thought you wanted to see your dad.'

'Oh, yes.' I smiled glassily at Helen and backed away. Oops, nearly . . .

Dad, puffing and red-faced, was unloading bottles of wine and beer from the car and taking them into the dining room.

'Shall we go and make sure the wedding cake's all ready?' I asked him. 'Mum wants us to take that to the hotel next – and then we've got to pick up the flowers.'

'It's all go,' he puffed. 'When am I supposed to

relax and enjoy myself?'

I reminded him that it was supposed to be the bride's day, not the bride's father's, and then Flicka and I went inside and put an enormous lot of sticky tape all over the wedding cake boxes, just in case anyone was tempted to lift the lids.

Mum was upstairs helping Helen with her so-called disaster as we set off for the hotel. Flicka was sitting in the front of the car, next to Dad, and I'd been rammed into the back seat with the three cake boxes.

'Now, I'm going to put the back seat belts round you and round the boxes,' Dad said, 'just to make them completely secure. Once that's done you're not to move, Katie.'

'Right,' I said gloomily. Not much chance of anything happening to the cake the way *he* was packing it . . .

'Mum's told you about the trampoline, has she?'

I nodded.

'Well, then . . . you're in the back in charge of this precious cargo, so if the tiniest thing happens it will be counted against you. You're not to move as much as a *eyelash*.'

'That's not fair!' I complained. 'Suppose I've just *got* to move. Suppose I get an uncontrollable urge to scratch my nose . . . or suppose I sneezed or something and all the cake boxes fell on to the floor — it wouldn't be *my* fault, would it?'

'It would most definitely be your fault,' Dad said severely. 'That wedding cake has cost me a small fortune and it's your responsibility to sit with it and guard it with your life. If there's a traffic accident or a fire, just remember: that wedding cake comes first.'

'Huh!' I said. 'It's nice to know that an old bit of fruit cake is more important that me.'

Dad got into the driver's seat, made sure Flicka had her seat belt on, and off we went, driving at about one mile an hour and stopping at green traffic lights as well as red. He got hooted at by other drivers and a woman went by us waving her fist, but he didn't take any notice.

We eventually arrived at Lichfield Manor Hotel. It was dead posh, all white columns and shiny brass, and outside there was a man wearing a red and black uniform who rushed to open our car doors.

'Shall I carry the boxes in?' I asked Dad. One last chance to trip up the steps . . . get caught in the revolving doors . . . fall headfirst over the carpet.

'Certainly *not*,' Dad said, handing box number one to the man with the uniform. 'You stay exactly where you are.'

Dad disappeared somewhere with Mr Uniform and I looked forlornly at Flicka. 'So much for that,' I said. 'What am I going to do now?'

She shook her head. 'I suppose you'll just have to own up,' she said. 'I'll come with you – we'll say we were mucking about and somehow you just fell on the cake . . .'

I nodded slowly. 'I'll just have to come right out and tell them. It's not that bad, is it? I mean, it's not as if I've ripped her wedding dress to pieces or set fire to the presents or anything. They can't *really* kill me.' And then I thought of Helen at her most menacing, of Mum and Dad as angry as dragons, of Mrs Bayleaf looming down on me, her face a fluorescent and angry pink to match her outfit . . . 'Well, maybe they can,' I said.

I nibbled thoughtfully on a bit of icing sugar that had somehow lodged itself under my fingernail. 'Let's go and see where the cake's going,' I said, getting out of the car. All right, I knew I'd have to confess when they found out, but it hadn't quite come to that yet.

Flicka and I swung round in the swing doors until some shouted at us, then set off in the direction of the Savoy Dining Room – I knew we were in there because there was a notice on the wall saying: *Bailey-Wilkins Wedding Party in the Savoy Room*. It was a huge room with the tables made into an 'E' shape, and they were already laid out with white cloths and a mass of knives, forks, glasses and bowls of blue and white flowers. On the top table there was a huge silver thing like a plate on legs.

'That's where the wedding cake sits,' Flicka said, pointing. 'And there's the big silver knife

they use when they pretend to cut it – for the photographs – and then the cake goes into the kitchens and they cut it all up properly.'

'They won't need to do that today,' I said. 'They'll be saved a lot of trouble.'

'Later, it comes back in little squares –'

'– or chunks and crumbs, as the case may be –'

'– and they give it to the guests and they sleep with it under their pillows and dream of who they're going to marry.'

'What if they're married already?'

'Dunno,' she said.

We peered round a corner and saw Dad talking to a man who looked like the manager. He was wearing a black jacket with tails and a spotted bow tie. We heard the words, 'wedding cake' and 'flowers' and 'champagne' and then Dad and he shook hands and Dad walked away.

'Now what?' Flicka whispered.

I thought quickly. I'd had an idea and it was worth a try. With Flicka trailing behind me, I approached Bow Tie.

'Excuse me, sir,' I said graciously. 'What a lovely hotel.'

He gave a slight bow. 'You like eet, madam?' he

said with a funny accent.

'Oh, we do!' I said. I cleared my throat. 'My friend and I are bridesmaids this afternoon. The next time you see us we'll be in whisper blue –'

'– with exquisite beading,' Flicka added.

He bowed again. 'I see. You are ze Bailey and Wilkins wedding in the Savoy Room, yes? And we also 'ave ze Jones family in the Ritz room. So 'ow may I be of service to you young ladies?'

'Well. That was my dad you were just speaking to,' I said.

'Ze fazzer of ze bride?' Bow Tie said.

'Yes. And I am ze . . . er . . . sizzer of the bride. And what my dad didn't tell you is that the bride . . . my sizzer . . . is allergic to wedding cake.'

He raised an eyebrow.

'Brings her out in a rash,' I said. 'Makes her sneeze and makes her nose run.'

'Oh dear,' he said. 'But why 'e not tell me zis?'

''E very absent-minded,' I said. I crossed my fingers. 'So what my muzzer told me to tell you was, could you leave bringing the cake out until the last moment. I mean, we don't want it in the room all the time on the silver plate thing.'

''Ow about if it was on ze far table?' he asked.

'No!' I said. 'No good at all. She can detect a wedding cake at fifty paces: her hair stands on end. She'll even be able to tell if it's out of its box anywhere in the hotel.'

He tutted. 'Oh dear. Poor madam.'

'So, we thought it would be best if you just brought it in at the very last minute, for the photographs.'

He bowed. 'Whatever madam wishes. When ze 'appy couple arrive, I shall tell them the wedding cake stay in anuzzer room.'

'No!' I said. 'Don't even *mention* it! She . . . she's so allergic to wedding cakes that you can't even say the word to her without her arms and legs swelling up.'

'Oh dear, oh dear,' he said. 'Poor, poor madam.'

Outside, we could hear Dad beeping his car horn.

'Got to go!' I said. 'Don't forget, will you?'

He gave me another bow. 'You and your muzzer and fazzer may rely on me.'

'There you are,' I said to Flicka as we hurried out. 'We've got another few hours.'

'I wish you wouldn't keep saying *we*,' Flicka said. 'It makes me really nervous.'

chapter four

'Mind the wall! Watch your step! Slowly, I said!'
Dad bellowed as I carefully carried a cardboard
tray of blue carnations into the house.

'I can manage,' I said with dignity. 'The way
you're going on, anyone would think I was
accident-prone.' I ignored the poke in the back

from Flicka, who was behind me carrying a tray of bouquets.

We laid all the flowers down on the kitchen table next to a plate of tiny dead fish on biscuits, then Helen, wearing a long white petticoat thing, and Mum, wearing her hairdo, rushed into the room.

'Oh! My flowers!' Helen said. 'Aren't they beautiful!'

'The money they cost, they ought to be,' muttered Dad.

Mum picked up an orchid and a bit of fern. 'Just look at my gorgeous corsage. They've managed to match my outfit exactly!' She whipped up the plate of dead fish. 'But fancy putting the flowers right next to the canapés, Richard!' she said, glaring at Dad. 'We'll all be going into church smelling of sardines.'

Dad, rolling his eyes and saying that he couldn't do anything right, went into the dining room to count bottles while Mum and Helen stayed oohing over the flowers.

'Look at these *sweet* little flower balls that you and Flicka will be carrying,' Mum said, holding up a blue and white lump – like a soap on a rope, only made of flowers.

'Lovely,' I said.

'We've been given Dorothy bags to carry as well,' said Flicka. 'They match our dresses.'

'Where on earth did you get those?' Helen asked sharply.

'Mrs Bayleaf brought them round,' I said. 'They were a surprise.'

Helen tutted. 'I do wish Mrs Bailey would keep her long nose out of everything,' she muttered to Mum. 'Every time that wo—'

'Little ears!' Mum said warningly, nodding towards me and Flicka, and Helen shut up.

'Has Mrs Bailey got her corsage?' Mum asked me.

I nodded. 'The shop said they'd delivered that – and Chistopher's and the best man's carnations – direct to their house.'

Mum looked at her watch. 'Only two hours to go!' she said, and Helen gave a scream and ran back upstairs.

Mum pulled down the kitchen blind, saying that the sun would make the flowers go limp.

'How did the cake look?' she asked me. 'Did it fit on its stand nicely?'

Out of the corner of my eye I saw Flicka moving slowly backwards out of the kitchen.

'They . . . they didn't take it out of its box while we were there,' I said.

'It's a beautiful cake,' Mum said fondly. 'It'll make a wonderful centrepiece for the table.'

I nodded. 'I expect it'll be a real talking point,' I said truthfully, then, 'Er . . . Mum?'

'What, love?'

'Are the people in that hotel all right?'

She paused from picking a greenfly off a carnation. 'What do you mean?'

'I mean, can they really be trusted – to look after the cake and everything properly?'

'Of course they can be trusted, silly. What d'you think they're going to do with the cake – pick it up and bowl it across the floor?'

'They might . . .' I said darkly.

'Don't be so ridiculous!' she said. There was a ring at the front door. 'That'll be your auntie and uncle. Go and let them in, Katie, and then go and look after Flicka.' She hesitated. 'She's a strange child, isn't she? Has she . . . er . . . mentioned anything else about wanting to do singing and dancing at the reception?'

I shook my head. 'I think she's gone off the idea.'

'Well, we can all be thankful for that,' Mum said.

I opened the door to Auntie Muriel and Uncle Brian and then went upstairs to Flicka, pausing on my way through to take four cheesey square things. I moved the others round on the plate to hide the gap; *that* was getting tricky because I'd eaten quite a few already.

Flicka had brought her pet mouse with her, so we fed him with the cheesey squares and, then, because he'd almost nibbled his way out of his cardboard box, found a big tin pencil box for him.

'Shall I take him to church in my Dorothy bag?' Flicka asked.

I shook my head. 'Better not,' I said. 'We're going to be in enough trouble with the cake.'

'But wouldn't it be *great*,' she said longingly. 'Just think if he somehow nibbled his way out of the Dorothy bag as we were going up the aisle, and ran up to see Mrs Bayleaf . . .'

The thought of a vast pink balloon jumping on a bench and shrieking was tempting, but I shook my head. 'It's all right for you,' I said gloomily. 'You haven't got to *live* here. I'm going to be killed enough for the cake, without him running up Mrs Bayleaf's leg.'

We sat and played with Mickey in my room, trying to teach him tricks and keeping well away from all the fuss and bother outside. It seemed that half the street was running up and down our stairs, calling to each other.

Suddenly it all went quiet, and then Mum called down the stairs, 'Richard! Come up here at once!'

'What have I done now?' I heard my dad mutter.

'There!' Mum said, when he reached the top. 'Doesn't our darling look a picture! Come and see, everyone!'

I opened my bedroom door to see Helen standing at the top of the stairs in her long white dress with the veil and sparkly tiara and train and everything. The whole bit. I smirked; she only

needed a magic wand and she'd have been the fairy godmother in Cinderella.

'You look beautiful, darling!' Mum said, dabbing her eyes. 'Doesn't she. Richard?'

'Beautiful,' Dad said, sniffing.

'Beautiful,' Auntie Muriel and Uncle Brian said, shaking their heads in wonder.

'Beautiful!' Helen's two friends said together.

Everyone looked at me and I looked straight back at them.

'Well?' Mum asked expectantly.

'Very nice,' I said.

'Like a fairy,' added Flicka, and then I shut the door and we both collapsed in giggles.

'Get your dresses on, you two!' Mum said, banging on the door. 'I'll be in there in a minute to help you do up your zips!'

Flicka and I looked at each other, rolled our eyes, then took the whisper-blue-with-exquisite-beading dresses off their hangers. I pulled off my tracksuit and struggled into the dress, stepped into the matching slippers and picked up my Dorothy bag. 'What do I look like?' I asked Flicka.

'A dog's dinner,' she said promptly.

Mum came in. 'There! You both look quite . . . er . . . lovely,' she said doubtfully. 'I'll just get Auntie Muriel in to see if she can do anything about your hair.' She moved in on me. 'You *have* had a bath this morning, haven't you, Katie?'

I crossed my fingers. 'What do you *think*?' I said indignantly.

'Only you smell a bit strange . . . a bit *mousy*,' Mum said, sniffing delicately.

'When are you getting out of that old thing and putting on your lovely new wedding outfit?' I asked her quickly, to change the subject.

She narrowed her eyes. 'This *is* it, Katie,' she said.

chapter five

At ten minutes to three Flicka and I were standing outside the church while last-minute wedding guests hurried through. Those that knew Flicka — those from her and Christopher's family — waved to her and said, 'You *do* look lovely!' or 'That colour really suits you!' but *my* relations just looked at me a bit alarmed and said, 'I never would have recognised you,' or 'I wondered who you were for a minute!'

I stared at them all, stony-faced. I hadn't *wanted* to be a bridesmaid; I'd never *asked* to be one. If they hadn't made me be a bridesmaid then I wouldn't have fallen on the cake. I hated my dress; the exquisite beading itched, the material was too tight across the chest and cut me under the arms, and whenever I tried to walk the swishy long skirt got trapped between my legs and deliberately tried to trip me up. The colour was sickening, the style was embarrassing and all things considered it was obvious that Mrs Bayleaf had left no stone unturned in her search to find the most ghastly bridesmaids' dresses in the whole world.

We stood there, swinging our blue and white flower lumps and trying to hide our Dorothy bags, waiting for Helen to arrive so we could put her veil straight and fluff out her train – or it might have been the other way round. Outside with us were a couple of ushers – Christopher's friends – who were giving out carnation buttonholes, also the photographer and a few assorted passers-by. After a while

we were joined by the vicar, looking worried.

He moved towards the ushers and I moved with him, wondering what was up. 'There might be a slight delay before the ceremony,' he said to the photographer in a low voice. 'The bridegroom isn't here yet.'

I let out a squeal. Christopher not here! The wedding would have to be cancelled! They wouldn't find out about the cake after all!

'Do you mean . . . do you mean he's left her waiting at the aisle – *abandoned* her?' I gasped.

'Hardly left her at the aisle,' one of the ushers said to me witheringly, 'because she's not here yet either, is she?'

I pulled a face at his back. That was just the sort of thing he *would* say – he was a teacher, same as Christopher. Everyone started looking at their watches, staring up and down the road and asking other people what the traffic had been like.

'Christopher's not coming,' I whispered to Flicka. 'He's changed his mind!'

'How do you know?' she whispered back.

'Just guessing.' I rolled my eyes dramatically. 'Helen's been jilted, abandoned! She'll have to go in a convent!'

Flicka screwed up her nose. 'Why does she have to do that?'

'Because you just do. I saw someone in a film once and when she was left at the aisle she went abroad to be a nun and work with poor people.'

'I don't think you have to do that nowadays,' Flicka said. 'And anyway, I shouldn't be so pleased about it – if they don't get married you won't be able to move into that nice big bedroom of hers, will you? *And* you'll have to give Christopher back his DVD player.'

I was quiet for a moment. 'Hadn't thought of

that,' I said.

There was a sudden movement from the people waiting outside the church and a shout of 'Here she comes!' and then the big black car holding Helen and Dad pulled up at the kerb with its white ribbons fluttering.

'I'll tell her!' I said, pushing myself forward. 'I'm her sister so it's got to be me who tells her. I'll just say he hasn't turned up so she'll have to go into a convent and help poor –'

'That won't be necessary,' interrupted the vicar, sweeping forward. He opened the passenger door of the car, spoke to Dad. 'There's a very slight delay,' I heard him saying in a low voice, 'so if you wouldn't mind just driving round the block . . .'

We all watched as the bridal car moved off. 'If there wasn't a wedding, would I still get the trampoline, d'you think?' I asked Flicka.

'Shouldn't think so,' she said. 'Especially when they found the cake.'

'They wouldn't find it, though, would they?' I said. 'It would go straight back to the shop for a refund.'

'They don't do refunds on things like wedding

cakes,' she said. 'It's not like finding you've bought the wrong packet of washing powder.'

'Anyway, I definitely think we ought to start telling people,' I said, 'then they can all collect their wedding presents before they go home.'

'I don't think . . .' Flicka began, and then the two ushers suddenly let out a big cheer and a second later a car containing Christopher and his best man pulled up at the kerb. I didn't know whether to be pleased or not.

'Blasted car wouldn't start!' Christopher said, jumping out. 'Had to go and find jump leads –

and then Mike forgot the ring and we had to go back for it.'

'Just as long as you're here now,' the vicar said soothingly, leading them off down to the front of the church.

After a moment or two Helen and Dad came back and we did the veil and train bit, and then the organ in the church started playing 'Here Comes the Bride' sort of music and we followed her down the aisle.

I can't remember much about the next bit, except that I was so busy waving to various aunties and uncles that I forgot to take Helen's bouquet when I was supposed to and she had to

turn and say, 'Katie! For heaven's sake!' in a very nasty voice and jab me in the exquisite beading.

After that came a boring bit in the vestry with people kissing each other, signing registers and saying, 'It was a gorgeous ceremony; absolutely lovely!' and me saying, 'There nearly wasn't one! I didn't think he was going to turn up, did you?' and everyone ignoring me.

When we got outside, the photographer took

about a million pictures: Helen and Christopher looking at each other, touching each other, holding hands with each other, kissing each other, and then Helen and Christopher doing all that all over again with Mr and Mrs Bayleaf, and then all over again with Mum and Dad and then again with me and Flicka and finally with everyone else in the church.

As Flicka and I, bored to bits, played helicopters by twirling our Dorothy bags round our heads, Mrs Bayleaf bore down on us.

'You look *adorable*,' she gushed. 'A pigeon pair!' She frowned slightly. 'But I wouldn't do that with your lovely bags or you'll spoil them!'

'That would be a pity,' I muttered quietly.

'And I've got another lovely surprise for you!' she said. 'There are two matching outfits for you to change into waiting at the hotel! Two gorgeously trendy dresses!'

We smiled at her glassily. 'I can hardly wait,' I said.

chapter six

'Well, you *have* got a good appetite, dear,' Gran said to me as I tucked into my third ice-cream sundae. We were in the Savoy Room and had nearly finished the wedding breakfast, which hadn't been a breakfast at all, but just an ordinary old roast dinner.

'It's just nice to have food again,' I said, forcing five cherries into my mouth. 'It's been *months* since we had proper meal at home – all Mum's been doing is fiddling around getting ready for the wedding.'

'Ah well, these things take some organising,' she said. 'There's the cars to see to and the flowers and the dresses and the cake and the . . .' She paused. 'That's strange. Where is the cake?'

I stopped cramming. 'Er . . . I expect they're saving it until last. Bringing it in for a surprise,' I said.

Gran craned her head to look up and down the long top table we were sitting on. 'They don't usually,' she said. 'It usually stands right in the centre of things. How very strange. I wonder if I ought to have a word with your mum to see if –'

'No!' I said. 'Don't do that.'

'But everyone's finished eating now. I'll just pop over and –'

'I'll go!' I said. 'Save you the trouble! I'm a bridesmaid, so I ought to do the errands. Save your legs!'

'There's nothing wrong with my legs,' Gran

said indignantly.

'Be right back!' I said, taking another gollop of ice cream.

Picking up metres of whisper blue skirt and tucking it into my knickers, I made my way along to Mum at the other end of the table. I didn't know how I'd got away with things for so long, actually, but there had been so much going on since we'd got to the hotel, what with everyone eating, drinking, kissing each other and saying what a *wonderful* day it was or what a *marvellous* meal and they hadn't seen each other for absolute *years*, that somehow no one had actually noticed that in front of where Helen and Christopher were sitting there was a great big silver plate with nothing on it.

I reached Mum and smiled at her. 'Your hair looks nice, Mum,' I said.

'I thought you didn't like it,' she said suspiciously.

'It's grown on me.'

Faintly, above the clamour, I heard Gran's voice calling, 'Just ask where the wedding cake is!'

I coughed to drown the last bit. 'Gran wants to

know where the wedding ... er ... hake is,' I said.

Mum looked mystified – as well she might. '*Hake?* What's a wedding hake?'

'A fish, I think,' I said. 'She just told me to ask you where the hake was. I think that's what she said,' I added innocently.

'Wedding hake ... ?' Mum's face was a picture of confusion.

'I think,' I whispered, 'that's she's had too many glasses of champagne.' I suddenly clapped my hand to my mouth, 'Oh, I get it – she doesn't

mean *hake*, she means *salmon*. That great big poached thing you've got at home.'

Mum's face cleared. 'Oh, of course. Just tell her it's for later. When we get back to our house.' I started off. 'Oh, and Katie . . .'

'What?'

'Take your dress out of your knickers, darling. It doesn't look very nice.'

Grudgingly, I pulled it out.

She patted my arm. 'You're being very good. Absolutely perfect.'

'*Am* I?'

She nodded. 'I know you're not enjoying it, but it's not for much longer – you're halfway to that trampoline already.'

Giving a hollow laugh, I went back along the row to Gran.

'Well?' she asked.

'Mum said . . .' I looked up and down the table in dismay; one of the waitresses had removed what was left of my sundae. 'Mum said it's for later,' I said, 'when we get back to the house.'

'It can't be!' Gran said. 'The wedding cake is always cut right after the speeches. It's traditional! Go back and –'

'Katie!' Mrs Bayleaf suddenly boomed behind us, making us both jump. No one would ever think a person made of candy floss could be so loud. '*There* you are! While there's a gap in the proceedings I want you and Felicity to come with me and see your gorgeous little dresses!'

Gran turned away with pursed lips – I knew she didn't like Mrs Bayleaf.

'Do we have to?' I muttered.

'What, dear?'

'Do we have to go and see them right now,

58

Katie means,' I heard Flicka say, hidden behind the bulk. 'In the middle of everything.'

'Oh, I think so, dear. Then you can be looking forward to putting them on, can't you?'

Reluctantly, we allowed ourselves to be led off. The dresses were in the bedroom that Helen and Christopher were using later to change into their going-away-on-honeymoon outfits. They were waiting in the wardrobe and when Mrs Bayleaf opened the door they sort of sprang out and hit us. They were bright yellow nylon, with fringes round the hem and zig-zag black along the front. Flicka and I started at them, aghast.

She beamed at us. 'All the go, these are!' she said, doing a sort of dance step on the spot. 'Groovy gear for discos, eh? And they've got matching jackets!'

The jackets were yellow nylon, too, with zips up the front and *Gissa Kiss!* embroidered in sequins on the back.

We were almost speechless with horror. 'But . . . but . . .' I managed after a moment.

'No!' Mrs Bayleaf protested. 'Don't thank me! I know the sort of gear you young girls like. I said

to myself, young Katie and little Felicity will *love* those!'

Silent, brooding on our fate, we went downstairs again, and when we got back into the Savoy Room they were just about to start the speeches.

'Haven't been able to get over and chat to your mum!' Gran said as I sat down. 'Auntie Maureen's been sick in the loo and I had to go and look after her. Maybe you could . . .'

But it was time for the speeches to begin.

Christopher rose to his feet. 'My wife and I . . .' he began, and everyone laughed, though I couldn't think why. 'My wife and I want to say a big thank you to everyone, and then Helen's dad is going to speak, and then we're going to cut the cake and –'

He suddenly stopped dead. 'Cake!' he said in a startled voice, looking at the empty silver plate.

'Cake!' Mum, Dad, Helen and Mrs Bayleaf said in startled voices altogether.

'Cake!' everyone else echoed.

Gran looked aggravated. 'I *kept* asking where it was but no one took any notice.'

I jumped up. 'I'll ask!' I said. 'I'm a bridesmaid, so I'll go and ask!'

'I think I'd better,' Dad said.

'No, let her go,' Mum said. 'It's good for her to be a bit responsible. Leave it to her!'

I smiled a sickly smile around the room as I made for the door. 'Yes, just leave it to me, every-one . . .'

chapter seven

I closed the door to the Savoy Room firmly behind me. It was crunch time . . . the time when I either had to own up and face everyone – or run away to sea.

I walked towards the main reception area of the hotel, thinking deeply, wondering if there was anything I could possibly do to stop them finding out what I'd done. Like, could I stick the good bits of the cake together? Or maybe get some of that dry ice stuff they use on stage to make everything look ghostly, so that no one could see it properly, or maybe there was a handy hypnotist around: *'When I count one-two-three everyone will see a beautiful wedding cake on the silver plate in front of them . . .'*

I realised that the chances of coming across the odd hypnotist wandering about were remote, so, sighing deeply, I went through the main lounge of the hotel where the guests for the other wedding party were gathering.

Totally ignoring a bridesmaid wearing a pink dress which was almost – but not quite – as revolting as mine, I was still thinking deeply when I bumped into Bow Tie, the man we'd spoken to that morning.

'Ah! The leetle bridesmaid sizzer of the bride!' he said, flouncing his tails behind him.

'That's right,' I said despondently.

'Are ze guests ready for ze wedding cake, then?'

'Afraid so,' I said. 'I've come to get it.'

He bowed and offered me his arm. 'Then we go

to ze kitchens togezzer and get ze beautiful cake
and zen we wheel eet in and everybody cheer!' he
said.

I looked at him gloomily. 'Not quite,' I said.
'What happens is we go to the kitchens together
and wheel in a load of cake crumbs and then
everyone grabs hold of me and kills me.'

A look of confusion spread over his face.
'Pleeze?' he said.

I sighed. 'I might as well tell you,' I said as we
walked down the corridor. 'You see, this morning
at home, I sort of fell on the wedding cake.'

A shock-horror look crossed his face. 'Sort of *fell* on it?!'

I nodded. 'Squashed it to bits. Demolished it. Zonked it good and proper.'

'But . . . but . . .'

'It's true,' I said, and went on in a rush, 'so then we — Flicka and I — decided that we'd put it all back in the boxes and get it here, and hope that an accident would happen to it on the way — but it didn't. And then I only pretended to you about Helen being allergic to cake so you wouldn't put it on display. And *then* Mum promised me a trampoline if I was a really good bridesmaid, and then everyone was busy eating their dinner so they didn't notice, but then they suddenly did, and now I've been sent out to get it,' I finished breathlessly.

'But . . .'

'So unless you've got a bucket of dry ice or a hypnotist or a . . .'

'Well, I never!' he suddenly said. 'You're in a right two and eight, aren't you?'

I looked up at him in surprise — he'd lost his foreign accent. 'What?'

'I never heard a story like that!' he said.

'Working here I've heard some wedding day tales, I can tell you, but I've not heard anything like *that* before. No, as far as I can remember, no one has ever fallen on her sister's wedding cake.'

'Why are you talking ordinary?' I asked suspiciously.

He clapped his hand to his mouth. 'Oops!' he said. 'In all the excitement I forgot me accent.'

'You aren't really foreign?'

He shook his head. 'Nah, I'm from London,' he said, 'but the punters like a Continental head waiter, see. It makes them feel they're getting a special service.'

I nodded. For all I cared he could have come from Mars.

Suddenly, in the corridor that led along to the kitchen, he stopped dead.

'Now look here,' he said. 'You know a secret about me – right?'

I nodded.

'And I know a secret about you. So you don't tell about me being as British as your auntie Doris and I won't tell about the cake.'

'Haven't got an auntie Doris,' I said. 'And anyway, it doesn't much matter about *me* because they're going to find out anyway.'

'Hmm . . .' he said thoughtfully.

There was something in that *hmm* that made me open my eyes very wide. 'There's nothing . . . I mean, you can't think of anything to save me, can you?' I asked, hardly daring to hope.

'Maybe . . .' He stepped behind a potted palm. 'Now look here,' he said in a hoarse whisper. 'You know there's another wedding?'

I nodded.

'Well, they're not eating yet. They're still at the

dry-sherry-at-the-door and kiss the mother-in-law bit.'

'Yes?' I said breathlessly.

'Well, all wedding cakes are more or less the same, so what if I sort of *borrowed* their wedding cake for a few moments – long enough for your happy couple to have their photos taken . . .'

'Ooh yes!'

'And then whisked it away saying it had to be cut up in the kitchen –'

'And use the real one for that! Which won't

need much cutting up,' I added.

'Quite,' he said. 'But is your one square or round?' he suddenly asked urgently.

I thought. 'Round,' I said. 'At least it was in the beginning.'

'Phew! So's the other one.'

My smile stretched right across my face; I might get away with it yet. Why, I could almost feel myself bouncing gently on my trampoline.

'I'll set it all up,' he said. 'You go off and tell your family that the cake is on its way.'

Hitching up my skirt I ran as fast as I could down the corridor towards the Savoy Room. Halfway there I remembered something and ran all the way back again to shout to Bow Tie to remember to put our own smirking little bride and groom – the ones Mum had spent about six months choosing – on top of the borrowed one.

He gave me a thumbs-up. 'Leave it to me, ducks,' he said.

chapter eight

I went straight back to the Savoy Room and when I opened the door everyone stopped chatting and drinking, and looked at me expectantly.

'It's OK!' I said airily. 'It's perfectly all right. The wedding cake is on its way.'

'Well, thank goodness for that,' Mum said.

'It should have been here all the time,' Gran said with a sniff. 'Did they say why it wasn't?'

I shook my head and muttered something about not having asked.

'I was beginning to think something must have happened to it,' she added.

I gave a false burst of laughter which was so loud that it made an old aunt of Christopher's shudder with fright. 'How could anything have *happened* to it?' I blustered. 'I mean, it couldn't have got *lost* or anything, could it? No one could have *fallen* on it or anything, could they?'

Flicka tugged at my arm urgently. 'I should stop right there,' she whispered. 'Come over in the corner here and tell me what's happened. Is there really a wedding cake coming? I haven't got to start singing to distract people, have I?'

We formed a small huddle of whisper blue in the corner and I filled her in on old Bow Tie's brilliant idea. Just as I'd finished explaining, the double doors of the room flew open and he came in pushing the wedding cake – well, not *the* wedding cake, *a* wedding cake – on a shiny silver trolley.

As three tiers of frosty white icing came into

view I sighed with relief. 'Look, it's all right,' I whispered to Flicka. 'I'm going to get that trampoline after all . . .'

For a good five seconds I pictured myself bouncing and turning somersaults, and then I noticed something about the cake, something drastic, and the trampoline disappeared in a flash and I crashed to the ground. You see, the cake now on display to the Bailey-Wilkins Wedding Party had little pink rosebuds all round the edges. *Pink rosebuds!* When it should have had bluebirds of

happiness!

I tried to breathe normally in my tight exquisite beading, hoping and praying that no one else had noticed. It might be all right, because hardly anyone had seen the cake except our family . . .

'Ooh!' everyone said as it came fully into view. 'What a picture! Beautiful cake! Three cheers for the wedding cake!' But Flicka said, '*Pink rosebuds!*' under her breath.

Bow Tie stopped and gave a bow. 'Perhaps ze leetle sizzer of the bride and her friend would like to wheel the cake to ze 'ead of ze tables,' he said.

Flicka went to leap forward but I grabbed hold of her. 'I'm not going anywhere near that cake,' I said under my breath.

'Why not? We are bridesmaids . . .'

'I know,' I said, out of the corner of my mouth like a ventriloquist, 'but me and wedding cakes don't mix. I'll probably go over there, trip on the trolley and send the whole lot rocketing up the corridor.'

'All right,' she said grudgingly.

'You can have first go of my trampoline, instead.' I waved to Bow Tie. 'It's OK,' I said. 'You can do it!'

He slowly wheeled the cake and trolley towards
Helen and Christopher. Everyone nodded at it
approvingly as it passed them. Everyone except
Mum – *she* looked at it and frowned. My heart
sank. She must have noticed!

I whizzed over with a bottle of champagne.
'More fizz, Mum?' I said quickly, standing between
her and the cake. 'You'll need some for the toast!'

'We now 'ave the ceremonial cutting of the cake
for ze photographs!' Bow Tie announced. 'If ze 'appy
couple would 'old 'ands togezzer wiz ze knife . . .'

Helen, giggling in a silly way, came out from

behind the table with Christopher and they stood, knife poised, over the cake.

'Hang on!' came a chorus of voices, as aunties and uncles scrabbled under the table and in their bags for their cameras.

Everyone gathered round them and a firework night of flashes went off. Back in my seat next to Gran I watched anxiously: don't get too near that cake, anyone . . . don't really cut it, Christopher . . . don't cough all over it, Auntie Jean, it's not ours . . . I shot another look at Mum. She'd moved her chair right back to see the cake better and was peering at it as if she couldn't quite believe her eyes. I'd have to try and distract her . . .

Before I could do that, though, Helen cooed that she wanted a photograph of the two of them standing by the cake with the bridesmaids. 'They've been so *good*,' she added fondly.

I smiled a sickly smile and stood as far back from the cake as possible – certainly out of falling distance – while still being in camera shot.

'Eef everyone is done,' Bow Tie said then, bowing, 'I now take ze cake for ze cutting up. We serve it wiz coffee in a few moments.'

'Yes, yes, I think everyone's done,' I said bossi-
ly. 'I should take the cake away quickly before it
melts.' I dashed to the door to open it for him,
filling Mum's glass with more champagne on the
way back to my seat.

'What I'd like to know is why it wasn't in here
before,' Gran said when I sat down. 'Fine state of
affairs, if you ask me. In my day the wedding cake
was always on show for the whole of the meal.'

'They do things differently nowadays, Gran,' I said. 'More champagne?'

'Hardly seen the cake, I haven't,' she grumbled. 'Big money they cost, too. I'm going to ask your dad to mention it to the management.'

'Do you like this stuff?' I said hastily, filling her glass so that bubbles ran over the top. 'I think it's like washing-up liquid. Mrs Bayleaf likes it, though. Flicka said she's on her fourteenth glass!'

Gran sniffed, rolled her eyes towards Mrs Bayleaf's bulky form. 'I'm not surprised. The size of her – I expect it goes down without touching the sides.'

'She's like a pink elephant, isn't she?' I said, moving slightly in front of Gran so that she wouldn't see the cake disappearing out of the door.

'More like a camel,' Gran said with a snort. 'More like a camel stocking up the old larder before it goes into the desert.'

This thought so amused her that she chortled her way through another glass of champagne and forgot all about the cake.

Mum didn't, though. Everyone had started pushing their chairs back from the tables and getting into little groups to chat, when she beckoned me over.

'Katie . . .' she said in a puzzled voice.

'More champagne, Mum?' I asked quickly, waving the bottle I'd brought with me. 'Do you want me to go round filling everyone's glasses?'

'No, thank you,' she said. 'With what we're being charged for that, it's time they moved on to coffee. No, I was just thinking about that cake . . .'

'Lovely, wasn't it?' I said quickly. 'And I liked the way he brought it in at the last minute . . . as if it was a special surprise.'

'But there was something strange about it,' she said. 'Only I can't think what it was. I tried to get close to have a good look but everyone was in the way, and then when he was wheeling it out I tried to stop him, but he ran the trolley over my toe.'

'I'm sure he didn't mean to!' I said in a shocked voice.

'Maybe not, but . . . that cake, Katie . . .'

We were back where we started. 'Yes, lovely, wasn't it? And I liked the way he . . .'

'No!' she said, holding up her hand. 'I've just realised what's wrong. It had *pink rosebuds*!'

chapter nine

'P-pink rosebuds?' I said, seeing my trampoline disappear so far into the distance that it vanished. 'Where?'

'All round! Decorating the tops of the three tiers!' Mum said. 'Of *course*. I *knew* there was something wrong.' She began to get up. 'I'm going to

find the manager. They've given us the wrong cake!'

'Surely not!' I said, playing for time. 'How *could* they have done?'

'I don't know,' Mum said grimly, 'but I intend to find out.'

'Just a sec!' I said, squashing myself into the chair next to her and blocking her way out. I crossed my fingers. 'I don't remember seeing any pink rosebuds.'

'Of course you do! You *must* have seen them. All round the top, they were.'

'I thought they were birds. Bluebirds! Are you sure your eyes are all right?'

'There's nothing wrong with my eyes!' Mum said sharply.

'They were a *pinky* sort of blue, mind you,' I said thoughtfully. 'And the birds were sort of roundish. A bit flower shaped.'

'Katie,' Mum said sternly. 'I know that as far as you're concerned I've got one foot in the grave, but I *do* know the difference between a *pink* rose and a *blue* bird.'

'Of *course* you do,' I said soothingly. 'It's just they were a pinkish sort of blue and what with the lights in here *and everything else* I thought you might have got muddled.'

'What do you mean – *and everything else?*' Mum said.

'Well, they looked perfectly all right to *me*. But then I haven't been drinking champagne,' I said meaningfully.

Mum hesitated, sank back in her seat. 'Did they *really* look like bluebirds to you?' she asked in a puzzled voice.

I nodded. 'Pinkish, rose-shaped bluebirds.' I

uncrossed my fingers. 'Look, why don't you hang on until the pieces of cake come round with the coffee, then you can have a real good look. Close up.'

'Well, I . . .'

'You don't want to look silly. Not in front of Mrs Bayleaf . . .' I added persuasively.

'Hmm,' Mum said – just as the large person in question appeared in front of us with Flicka in tow.

'*Such* a wonderful day,' she gushed, pink chiffon quivering about her. 'My Christopher and your Helen . . . so touching . . . such a marvellous ceremony . . .'

'Yes,' Mum said, 'but I was just talking to Katie about the wedding cake. Don't you think –'

'Don't you think it was perfectly *lovely*, Mrs Bailey?' I interrupted. 'And the way they brought it in at the last minute and – goodness, is that the time? I expect you want me and Flicka to go with you and change into our lovely outfits now, don't you?'

'That's right, dear,' Mrs Bayleaf said.

I jumped up. 'Straight away, Mrs Bailey,' I said

with a smarmy smile. 'And once we're wearing them perhaps we can help pass round the coffee and cake. *Cake with bluebirds on it*,' I added in a whisper to Mum as we went out.

Upstairs our yellow and black horrors were spread out on the bed and lying in wait for us. They looked even more horrific, somehow: the zips seemed zippier, the nylon shinier, the sparkly *Gissa Kiss* even sparklier.

Mrs Bayleaf held a jacket up in front of her. 'Well, aren't these the trendy rave?' she said. 'I know what you young girls like, don't I? Fab gear, eh?'

'Fab gear . . .' Flicka said faintly.

'Now, get yourselves out of those bridesmaids' dresses and then it's on with your trendy little outfits!'

I looked at Flicka and she looked at me. It was the only moment when I wasn't in a hurry to get out of whisper blue.

Five minutes later, red-faced, hating Mrs Bayleaf intensely and looking as if we'd escaped from the 1980s, we were back downstairs.

In the Savoy Room, things were buzzing – and the sight of us made Mum laugh so much that she quite forgot about the cake. 'Not so much losing a daughter as gaining a banana!' she spluttered, and I pretended to laugh, just to keep her mind off things.

All the tables and chairs in the room had been pushed back and Helen and Christopher were 'circulating', Mum said. This meant they were going round lying about people's presents ('Thank you so much for that marvellous vase,' I heard Helen say, when I'd overheard her only the day before telling Mum she'd never seen such a monstrosity in all her life and she was going to knock it off the shelf as soon as she possibly could).

Dad was chatting to a very pretty woman in a blue hat; I think she was one of Christopher's relatives. When I passed them on my way to see if there was anything left to eat on the big table, I heard Dad say, 'Of course, I still play a lot of squash. I don't believe in growing old gracefully. Oh indeed, I still put down a mean old game.'

When he saw me he stopped dead. 'My God, I thought you'd changed into a canary!' he said, and he gave a roar of laughter. 'This is my daughter Katie,' he said to the woman. 'Well, I say my daughter, though I don't feel there's much of a generation gap. I quite often get taken for her older brother, you know.'

I stared at him in amazement; what on earth was he going on about? 'Did you borrow Gran's corset in the end?' I asked.

'Wh . . . what?' he blustered.

'You know – Mum and Helen said you needed one. To keep your stomach in so you could get into that suit,' I said.

There was a moment's silence and then the pretty woman giggled. Dad gave a loud, false 'Ha ha!' of laughter and then said, 'Shouldn't you be going round talking to people, Katie? Don't let us keep you.' Bow Tie came in, wheeling the trolley, and he nodded towards the door. 'And anyway, it looks as if it's time to hand round the cake.'

I dashed over as quickly as my zips and sequins would allow.

'Everything OK?' I asked Bow Tie breathlessly.

He looked me up and down. 'Are you wearing that for a bet?'

'Don't blame me,' I said. 'It's all Mrs Bayleaf's fault. It's what is known as "a groovy rave outfit", apparently.' I looked anxiously at the trolley. 'Did you get the other cake back all right? Was there enough good bits of ours to cut up?'

He pointed to a huge white dish covered by a silver lid. 'Eef madame would care to leeft the lid . . .'

'Never mind all that French bit,' I said urgently. 'Is it all right?'

'*Voila*!' he said, bowing and whisking off the lid at the same time.

Heart in mouth, I stared at the dainty oblongs of wedding cake neatly placed in rows round and

round the plate: dainty oblongs of wedding cake –
with bluebirds of happiness on them!
Triumphant, gloating, bouncing a little as if I was
already on my trampoline, I carried the first piece
over to Mum . . .

chapter ten

The wedding day, as Dad had just remarked to everyone crowding into our sitting room, was almost over – all he had to do now was pay for it. Helen and Christopher had gone off on their honeymoon with a pile of tin cans and one of Mrs Bayleaf's pink shoes tied to the back of their car, and the rest of us – plus the extra relatives who hadn't been invited to the wedding proper – were at home and actually being *urged* to eat the food which Mum had been hiding from everyone for months.

Flicka was staying the night and she and I were doing our last bridesmaidly duties – taking nibbles from the kitchen and transferring them into the guests' ever-open mouths.

Mum, hair more or less flattened back to normal now, stood in the kitchen hacking bits off the turkey, trying to make the prawn vol-au-vents go round and pretending she'd made all the shop-bought quiches.

'Ask Gran if she'd like some salmon with her salad,' she said to me, 'and then go round collecting cups.'

Gran, standing in the doorway and chatting to Christopher's gran about when everyone had been babies, overheard. 'Yes, please, dear,' she said. 'I've been looking forward to having that. And a nice dollop of mayonnaise on the side, please, Katie.'

'And by the way – it's not *hake*!' Mum said to Gran. 'It's salmon!'

'Of course it's salmon,' Gran said. 'What else would be pink and have pieces of cucumber all round it. *Hake*? Of course it's not hake.'

Mum laughed. 'Then why, at the reception, did you ask where the hake was?'

'I never did!' Gran said indignantly. 'I might be getting on, but I do know the difference between . . .'

'Aaaghh!' I cried, clutching my tummy and reeling forwards.

'What's the matter?' Gran and Mum both said together.

'Terrible pain. Feel ever so sick. And faint,' I added for good measure.

'Too much excitement,' Gran said at the same time as Mum said, 'Too many ice-cream sundaes. Flicka, would you take Katie into the garden to get some fresh air, please.'

Flicka led me off, grinning, and I staggered to the door pretending to fan myself and holding my stomach at the same time.

There was a miracle cure once we were outside. 'Phew! That was close,' I said. 'I really thought Gran was going to drop me in it.'

Flicka shook her head doubtfully. 'I still don't know how you're going to get away with it. Your mum hasn't stopped puzzling about those blue-birds, you know.'

'Oh, it'll be OK,' I said airily. 'I'll get them to order the trampoline tomorrow and if anything gets discovered after that it'll be too late.' I walked down to the end of the garden. 'I think I'll have the trampoline here,' I said, pointing to the corner by the blackcurrant bush. 'Then when I'm practising my forward twists and get hungry I can grab a few currants as I bounce by.'

'You've been so *lucky*,' Flicka said. 'If they hadn't had Mr Bow Tie on duty . . .'

'I know,' I said. 'I told Dad to give him a good tip.'

'Your mum's face – when she finally got her piece of cake!' Flicka squealed suddenly.

'She had to borrow my dad's glasses and take it to the light and she *still* wouldn't believe they were bluebirds!'

We curled up laughing at the thought – and Mum immediately appeared in the kitchen doorway. 'I see you're feeling better then, Katie,' she said. 'You can come in and help hand round cups of tea now.'

'*More* tea!' I marvelled as we went in. 'How can they drink so much! Everyone's had at least a gallon since they got back.'

'Better that than a gallon of champagne,' Dad said, leaning in the doorway getting a breath of air. As we went past he said, '*Gissa Kiss*!' and roared with laughter.

We handed round about twenty teas and then we ran out of cups. 'You and Flicka had better go on washing-up duty,' Mum said to me. 'We can't start using our old chipped mugs in case Mrs Bailey sees them.'

I'd just started to object to washing-up and Mum had just started to remind me that I was supposed to behave wonderfully *all day*, when Auntie Muriel gave a shriek and rushed in with her hat on crooked.

'The photographs are here!' she said. 'Everyone's to come and choose the ones they want from the proofs.'

Mum, me and the rest of the world bundled into the hall and surrounded the girl from the photographers. 'Perhaps just two people could look at them at a time,' she said nervously. 'That way we won't get the orders muddled. Let's have the bride and groom's immediate family first, please.'

Mrs Bayleaf bulldozed her way forward and everyone else moved. 'Cedric and I will find a quiet little corner somewhere and have a *lovely* browse,' she said to Mum. 'I'll bring them to you next.'

'Oh, no hurry,' Mum said, rolling her eyes at Gran. She propelled me back into the kitchen and Uncle Brian slapped me on the back and said,

'*Gissa Kiss*!' as we went through.

'Of course, there'll only be the ones taken at the ceremony there,' Mum said thoughtfully, filling up the sink with water. 'The official photographer had gone by the time they cut the cake.'

My hand, halfway through stuffing a strawberry tart into my mouth, stopped dead.

'It's those ones I *really* want to see,' she said, 'but I suppose I'll just have to wait until someone in the family gets their snaps developed.'

'What do you want to see those for, then?' I asked.

'To look at the cake, of course,' she said, standing me firmly in front of the sink. 'To have a really good look at those bluebirds.'

I gave a nervous laugh. 'You won't be able to see little things like that properly,' I said. 'And anyway, when you use a flash people always come out with red eyes, don't they?'

'So?'

'So . . . that's what a flashlight does – makes things look red. And pink. I just bet in those photographs that the bluebirds look pink!'

Mum looked at me sharply while squirting a jet

of washing-up stuff into the sink. 'There's more to this than meets the eye, Katie,' she said, 'and I can't help thinking that you've got something to do with it.'

I smiled uneasily. 'Shall I go round collecting more cups before I start washing?'

'Yes, do that,' she said.

'And Mum?'

'What?'

'Don't you think, if I'm going to wash up, I ought to get out of this *lovely* outfit in case it gets spoilt?'

'All right,' she said. 'But Katie – none of your old tracksuits. Just a nice skirt and blouse, please.'

I told Flicka we could change and we dashed upstairs, found something to wear – and brought Micky downstairs with us in a Dorothy bag.

'Just in case Mrs Bayleaf takes too long over the photographs,' I said.

We slid down the stairs as best we could (there were people all over them) and went into the kitchen.

'Here we are all ready to wash up!' I said to Mum, who was engrossed with something in the corner. 'I am being good, aren't I? I think I'm *being* perfect. When are you going to order the trampoline? Can Flicka come over next weekend and stay and then she can have a . . .'

Mum turned round, a strange expression on her face. 'Katie,' she said. 'What's this?' She held up my old pink tracksuit. 'And more to the point – why is it absolutely covered in wedding cake?'

Out of the corner of my eye I saw Flicka and her Dorothy bag slipping quietly out of the kitchen.

I sighed wearily. 'Oh dear,' I said. 'It's a long story . . .'